Shadows of Life

Birth, Life, Death... Infinity

ESTEBAN

Books Academy LLC
112 SW H K Dodgen Loop, Temple, Texas 76504
Hotline: (254) 800-1189

Ordering Information:
Quantity sales. Special discounts are available on quantity purchases by corporations, associations, and others. For details, contact the publisher at the address above.

Printed in the United States of America.

ISBN-13: Softcover   978-1-966567-92-9
          Hardbound   978-1-966567-93-6
          eBook   978-1-966567-94-3

Library of Congress Control Number: 2025913805

Introduction

A pencil saved my life. Born into a world of poverty, surrounded by uncertainty, I grew up in a family where self-worth was an unfamiliar concept. I was the fourth of twelve children, each of us carrying names that did not always belong to our true lineage. My mother bore her children to nine different men, and many of us never knew our fathers. In a home where survival overshadowed dreams, there was little room for identity, and even less for vision.

But from an early age, I carried something within me—a quiet, persistent voice that guided me, urging me to observe, to analyze, to make sense of the world around me. My mind captured moments like a camera, imprinting every struggle, every triumph, every feeling of isolation. And then, at four years old, I picked up a pencil.

That pencil became more than a tool. It was my sanctuary, my compass, my salvation. With each stroke, I discovered the ability to translate the intangible into form. Art became my language when words failed. It became my shield in times of hardship, my bridge to understanding a world that often felt unwelcoming. Through my art, I shaped my identity, transformed my pain, and found purpose.

Now, seventy years later, my journey as an artist has not only been one of self-discovery but of spiritual awakening. Life has taught me that our time here is fleeting—we are temporary visitors in this world, but we are permanent members of what lies beyond. Shadows of Life is a reflection of this truth. It is an exploration of existence in its most profound form: birth, life, death... and the infinity that follows.

Through my art, I have become a Spiritual Warrior. This book is my offering—an invitation to step into the shadows, to contemplate the impermanence of life, and to recognize the eternal presence that awaits beyond.

Acknowledgement

I would like to express my profound gratitude to everyone who supported me throughout the process of writing and publishing this book.

First and foremost, I extend my thanks to my Author Advisor, Lexie White, whose untiring efforts and professional guidance were priceless in bringing this book to fruition.

I would also like to recognize the exceptional team at Books Academy. Their keen insight and meticulous attention to detail enhanced the quality of this book. The professional staff, including the design and marketing teams, were crucial in transforming a manuscript into a published book ready for readers.

Lastly, I thank the readers and supporters who have taken an interest in my work. Your engagement and feedback continue to motivate and inspire.

This book is not just a reflection of my vision but a collaboration of many brilliant minds and kind hearts who believed in this project.

Dedication

This book is dedicated to my family and the millions of families who struggle with prioritizing their children's needs. It is important to realize that each child has a dream, aspiration, or goal which enhances the substance of their lives.

I personally dedicate this book to my mother, Maebelle Mott Poindexter (Jezebel) and her husband, Daniel Eugene Poindexter (Hesychia); my half-sister, Melanie Freeman Richburg (Lilith) and her husband, Ronald Richburg (Samuel); and my half-brother, Timothy Dwight Daniels (Rasputin)

They say when life gives you lemons, make lemonade. I am very grateful for my family creating conditions which continue to inspire and motivate me.

Chapter 1:
The Illusion of Perfection

"Beauty meets the undead—where horror and allure dance in the moonlight."

ESTEBAN

"Beauty meets the undead—where horror and allure dance in the moon-light."

ESTEBAN

"A face etched in nightmares, whispering horrors from the abyss."

ESTEBAN

"Killer looks, deadly charm—beauty never dies."

ESTEBAN

"Deadly elegance—where horror meets haunting beauty."

ESTEBAN

Chapter 2:
The Truth Beneath the Surface

"Rising from the abyss, he brings the nightmare to life—Halloween's true har-binger of horror!"

ESTEBAN

"Beauty fades, but hunger lasts forever."

BEAUTY'S ONLY
SKIN DEEP
ESTEBAN

"The dead don't rest... they rise, hungry for the living."

"A gallery of the damned—where every stare follows you into the abyss."

ESTEBAN

"When the Jack-o'-lanterns glow, the undead gather for a feast beyond the grave!"

Safety Matches